Wake Up!

Katie Cleminson

For Bee and Bird

WAKE UP!
A RED FOX BOOK 978 1 862 30628 8

Published in Great Britain by Red Fox,
an imprint of Random House Children's Books
A Random House Group Company

This edition published 2010

1 3 5 7 9 10 8 6 4 2

Copyright © Katie Cleminson, 2010

The right of Katie Cleminson to be identified as the author and illustrator of this work has been asserted in accordance
with the Copyright, Designs and Patents Act 1988.

RANDOM HOUSE CHILDREN'S BOOKS
61–63 Uxbridge Road, London W5 5SA

www.kidsatrandomhouse.co.uk
www.rbooks.co.uk

Addresses for companies within The Random House Group Limited can be found at:
www.randomhouse.co.uk/offices.htm

THE RANDOM HOUSE GROUP Limited Reg. No. 954009

A CIP catalogue record for this book is available from the British Library.

Printed and bound in China

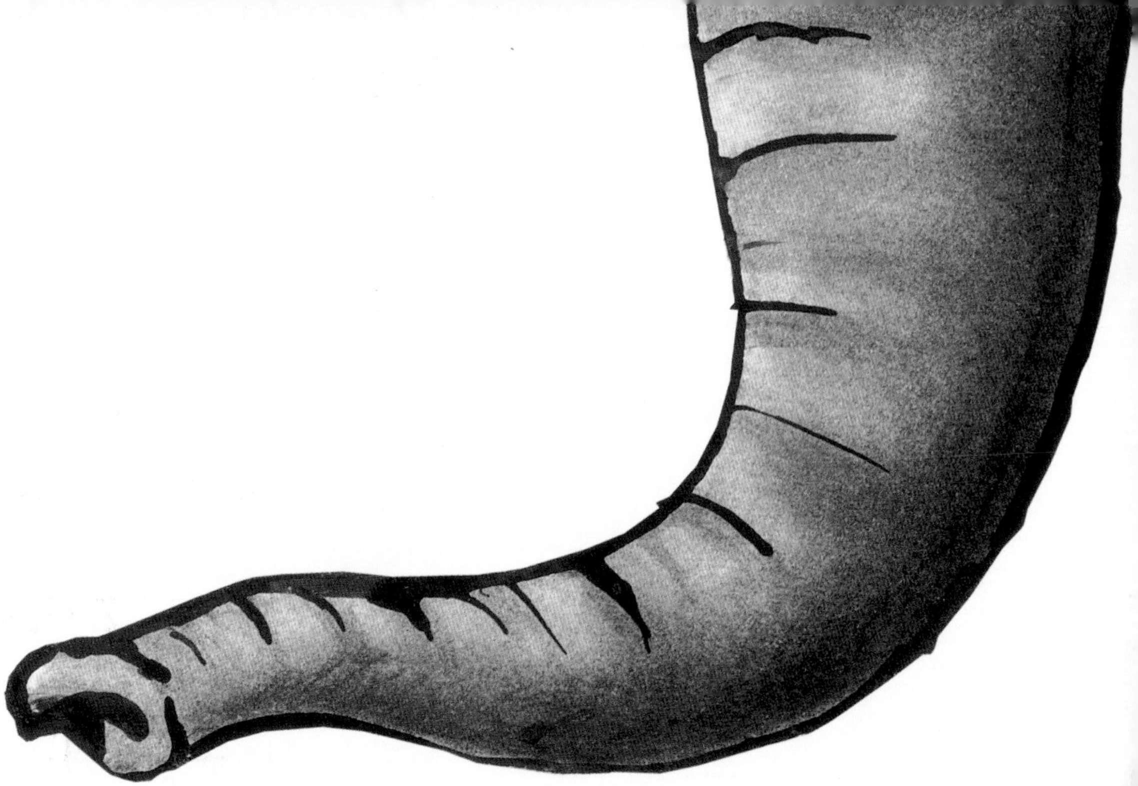

Wake up . . .

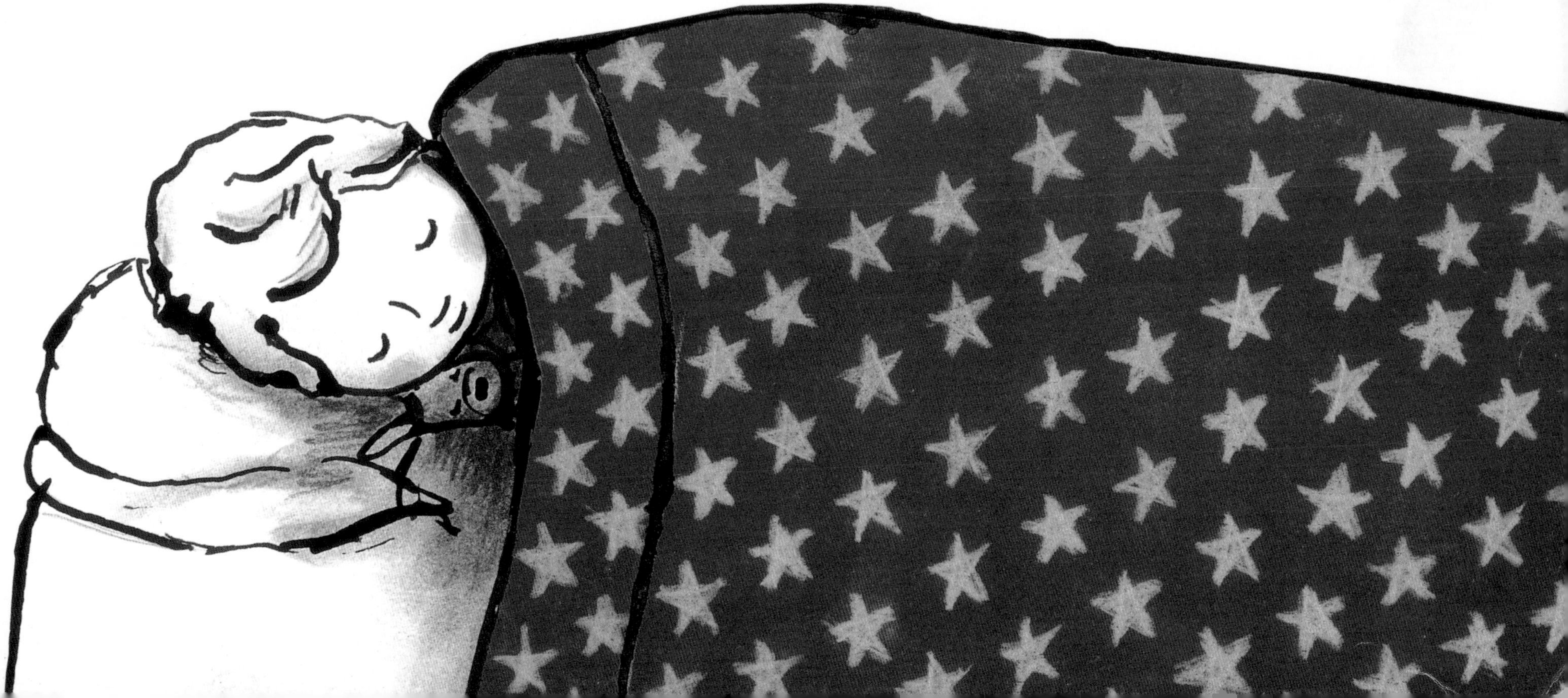

and up,

and up!

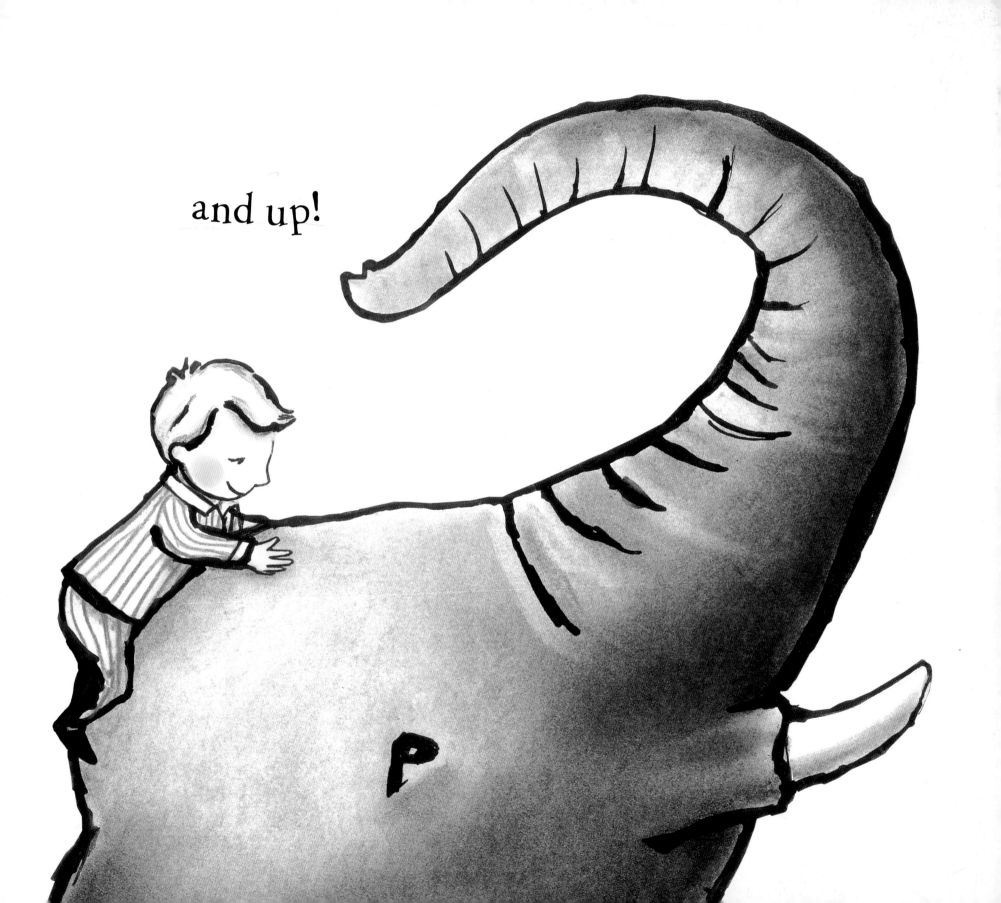

And stretch and scratch,

and scrub and wash,

comb your hair,

give teeth a brush.

It's time to dress.

Dress up . . . and up, and up!

Find pants and vests,

and shoes and socks,

and shorts and coats,
and favourite tops.

It's time for school.

Listen up . . .

and up,  and up!

And read and draw,

and count and spell,

ask and answer,

show and tell.

It's time to play.

Swing up . . .

and up,

and up!

And run and jump, and climb and slide,

sing and dance,   seek and hide.

It's time for dinner.

Eat up . . .

and up,

and up!

And chew and sip, and slurp and crunch,

use knife and fork,

and chomp and munch.

It's time to wash.

Clean up . . . and up, and up!

Then pick and choose,

and search and look,

and read aloud
    the perfect book.

            At last it's time to . . .

and up!

and up,

Cuddle up · · ·

Say goodnight,

yawn and stretch,

shut your eyes,

doze and rest . . .

It's time to dream . . .